USBORNE
LEARN TO PLAY
MOZART

Michael Durnin
Designed by Russell Punter
Illustrated by Peter Dennis
Series editor: Anthony Marks

Music arrangements by Daniel Scott

Music engraving by Poco Ltd.,
Letchworth, Herts

Contents

Mozart is one of the greatest composers who ever lived. This book is an introduction to his music, and a history of his life. It contains over twenty-five pieces. Most of them are very well known. Others may be less familiar because they are performed less often. You can follow Mozart's musical career as you go through the book, because the pieces appear in the order Mozart wrote them.

The pieces are arranged for piano or electronic keyboard, specially simplified to make them easier to play. Most of them are extracts of larger pieces. Some are taken from music Mozart wrote for the piano, but others are from pieces for orchestra or other combinations of instruments.

Most of the pieces have been arranged to be played by one person. But some of them have been written so that you can play them either on your own or with a friend, and one is for two players on one piano. For more about this, see the section called "Playing the pieces" on pages 60-61. Here you will also find hints about how to play each piece, and help with any parts that may be difficult. On page 62 there is a list of the most important events in Mozart's life. Musical terms, and some other words that may be unfamiliar, are explained in the glossary on page 63.

Naming Mozart's pieces

Some of the pieces in this book have numbers by their names. These are known as "K" numbers, and refer to a special catalogue of Mozart's music. You can find out more about this on page 38.

Mozart was born on January 27, 1756 in Salzburg, a town now in western Austria. He was given the name Joannes Chrysostomus Wolfgangus Theophilus Mozart, and called Wolfgang by his family. His mother, Maria Anna, had seven children, but five of them died while they were still small children. Wolfgang had one sister, who was five years older than him. She was also called Maria Anna, and known by the family as Nannerl.

Mozart at the age of 5

The Mozarts lived on the outskirts of Salzburg, on the third floor of a house owned by their landlord Johann Hagenauer. Wolfgang's father, Leopold Mozart, was a musician at the court of the Archbishop of Salzburg. The year Wolfgang was born, he published an important book about violin playing. By the time his son was seven years old, Leopold was deputy music master at the archbishop's court.

The cathedral at Salzburg, where Leopold Mozart worked.

A musical education

Wolfgang and Nannerl did not go to school. Leopold taught them at home, concentrating mainly on music. He realized very quickly that his children were extremely talented musicians. He wrote about their progress in his notebooks. Wolfgang's abilities were particularly surprising.

The first page of Leopold's book about the violin

At the age of four, Wolfgang could already play complicated pieces on the harpsichord or organ. At the age of five, he began writing short pieces of his own. He also had an astonishing memory for music.

Leopold knew that other people would also think his children were special. He believed that if they were given the opportunity, Wolfgang and Nannerl would impress audiences wherever they played. He decided to take them on a tour of Europe so that they could perform in public and at royal courts. He assumed that his children would grow up to be professional musicians like himself, and believed that meeting

The square in Salzburg where the Mozart family lived

important musicians would help their careers. He also hoped to make money from their performances, and wanted them to see the most famous cities in Europe. He decided to begin traveling while Wolfgang and Nannerl were still young enough to be considered special and unusual. Between 1762 and 1773, Wolfgang Mozart traveled all over Europe.

Mozart's names

"Theophilus" is Greek for "God-loving" or "loved by God". Mozart used this name in several languages, often signing himself in French (Amadé), Latin (Amadeus) or German (Gottlieb).

The family journeys

In 1762 Wolfgang, Leopold and Nannerl traveled to Munich in Bavaria (now part of Germany) and played at the palace of Nymphenburg. Later that year the whole family went by boat and carriage to Vienna, and performed for the imperial court at the palace of Schönnbrun. The children played for the Empress, Maria Theresia, and to Viennese aristocrats and important visitors from other countries.

This map shows the main musical cities of Europe in the 18th century.

It was necessary for the children to meet these people, but the largest musical cities of the time were London and Paris. So in 1763 the family set out in their own carriage on the first of several tours of Europe. In just over ten years, they visited and performed in all the cities on the map above.

The family spent a few weeks in Brussels, then five months in Paris. They played for the French king, Louis XV, and Wolfgang's music was published for the first time. They then stayed for 15 months in London. The children played for King George III, and at public concerts. During this time Wolfgang composed his first large pieces for orchestra. He was still only eight years old.

Wolfgang and Nannerl performed at the palace of Nymphenburg, Bavaria.

The return journey to Salzburg took more than a year, and included short stays in Belgium, the Netherlands and Paris.

A search for work

The family stayed in Salzburg less than a year before they went traveling again. They went back to Vienna, hoping that the Empress would offer Mozart work as a musician at her court. However this did not happen, and the family returned to Salzburg disappointed and short of money.

Leopold went back to work at the archbishop's court in Salzburg, but he was already planning his next trip. He had decided to take Wolfgang to Italy. Italy was the home of opera (see pages 40-41), as well as many other new ideas in music, such as the invention of the piano.

From December 1769 to March 1771 Leopold and Wolfgang travelled round Italy. The tour followed the pattern of the earlier ones. They stopped in all the major cities, where Wolfgang impressed the audiences with his abilities and learned from the greatest Italian musicians.

By 1773 Leopold and Wolfgang had made three trips to Italy. Wolfgang was asked to compose many pieces, and his performances made quite a lot of money.

Maria Anna

Mozart's sister Maria Anna, or Nannerl, was an excellent pianist. But after her success as a child, she rarely played in public. This is partly because in those days it was less common for women other than singers to become professional musicians.

Maria Anna

This is the portable keyboard that the family took with them on their travels.

But above all Leopold hoped that Wolfgang would be offered work at one of the imperial or royal courts. This would have given him a regular income and helped his career. When they were not offered work in Italy, they tried again to find a job for Wolfgang as a court musician in Vienna. But the Empress lost patience with them, and they were forced to return to Salzburg once more.

Gallimathias musicum

Gallimathias musicum means "musical jumble". It is a collection of short, witty pieces based on other people's music.

The Hague

Mozart wrote it while staying in The Hague, Holland, on the way back from England. He was nine years old.

Mozart's travels

Mozart spent about 250 days of his life on the road from city to city. He went by horse-drawn coach or carriage. The family stayed at inns, which were cold, damp and dirty, or sometimes at monasteries.

Leopold found the journeys uncomfortable and slow, but as a child Wolfgang found them exciting. On his trip to Italy with Leopold, he wrote to Nannerl about how the driver made the horses go as fast as possible on straight roads. Wolfgang performed on the keyboard or violin wherever they stopped.

This is the sort of coach that the Mozarts would have used during their travels in Europe. Public coaches like this ran between all the major European cities.

Gallimathias musicum contains imitations of bagpipes and horn-calls, and deliberately bad harpsichord pieces.

Prince William of Orange

It was written for Prince William of Orange, who was made heir to the throne of Holland while Mozart was there.

D.C. al Fine

A brilliant child

Many people who saw Mozart perform wrote about his skills. His abilities were very unusual indeed for such a young child. We know, for example, that he wrote his first pieces of music at the age of five. There are also stories of his ability to make up pieces on the spot (this is called improvisation) and to play even the most difficult pieces perfectly the first time he saw them.

After hearing long pieces of music only once he could play them perfectly from memory or write them down without

mistakes. He could also play a keyboard instrument with a cloth covering the keys. (This is not in fact as difficult as it looks, but it seemed very impressive to audiences at the time.)

He also had perfect pitch (the ability to name any note that was played without having to check it first on a keyboard). In return for entertaining people like this he was given gifts and money. Leopold sometimes claimed Wolfgang was a year younger than he actually was, to make him seem even more remarkable.

Senti l'eco

This aria is from Mozart's first opera*, *La finta semplice* ("The pretend fool"). Below you can find out more about arias.

La finta semplice was first performed at the archbishop's palace in Salzburg (left). Mozart was still only 13 years old.

Andante un poco adagio

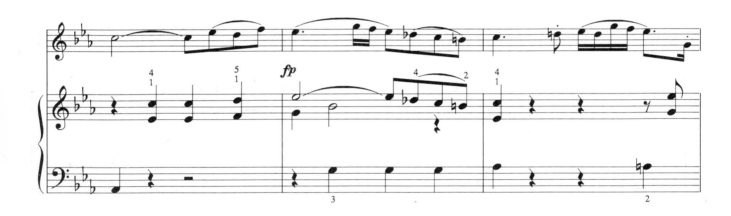

Songs and singers

In Mozart's time, the most common type of operatic song was the aria. Arias were sung by the main characters. The action stopped while they explained their thoughts and feelings. Arias also allowed singers to show off their skills, because they were often difficult to sing.

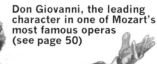

Don Giovanni, the leading character in one of Mozart's most famous operas (see page 50)

Find out more about opera on pages 40-41.

The top line can be played on the flute, recorder or violin. Or you can play the top and bottom lines on the piano alone.

The title means "I hear the echo". The top line imitates the keyboard, like an echo.

Guglielmo, a character from Mozart's opera *Così fan tutte*

People often went to the theater to hear the singers rather than the opera. Many singers became very famous and powerful, and were able to choose what they sang. If they liked a particular aria, they would often insert it into the opera they were appearing in, even if it had nothing to do with the plot.

from Lucio Silla

Lucio Silla is an opera based on the life of the Roman general Lucius Sulla, who is shown on this Roman coin.

Mozart wrote this piece shortly before he left Italy in 1772.

Music engraving

A lot of music these days, including the music in this book, is prepared by computer. In Mozart's day the process was very different. A craftsman had to engrave the lines, notes and symbols onto plates made of pewter (a soft mixture of tin and lead). The engraver used special tools to rule the lines and draw the slurs. The note heads were stamped with small chisels called punches.

Engraving the lines

Punching the notes

Lucio Silla was first performed in 1772, in the Teatro Regio Ducal, a theater in Milan.

After that it was not staged again until 1929, when people became interested in the early works of Mozart.

Music printing

To print the music, the engraved lines were filled with ink. Then paper was pressed on to the plate so that it made contact with the ink.

Some composers, including Leopold Mozart, had their own sets of punches to engrave music. Many of the shapes of musical notes and symbols we use today come from the styles of engraving and printing used in the 18th century.

Polishing the plates

Printing the music

Musical life in Mozart's time

Mozart's musical world was very different from his father's. Most musicians of Leopold's time had only two choices. They either became church musicians or worked in the palaces and courts of the royal family and other noblemen. Leopold expected his son to follow this sort of career, and encouraged Wolfgang to take this type of job.

Church music

Every cathedral and large church had a choir and an organist, and some had an orchestra too. The most important musicians at the archbishop's court in Salzburg were the chapel-master and his deputy. A few chapel musicians were chosen to become court composers. They helped the chapel-master choose and write the music to be played at church.

The cathedral at Salzburg

Music was needed on many occasions, especially on Sundays and religious festivals. The archbishop also often required music to impress important visitors. When there was no appropriate piece, a court composer was expected to write one. But he was not free to write exactly as he wished. He had to use words that were approved by the church, and set them to music in a style that would please the archbishop.

Music at the state courts

Many members of the royal family and other noblemen had their own palaces or courts. They needed music for many types of occasion. Court musicians had fewer restrictions than church musicians. Each court wanted to impress the others, so the music had to be grand and elaborate to display the skill of the composer and players. Court composers also often taught music to their employers and their children, and wrote music for them to play.

When he became a court composer, Mozart wrote many pieces for his employers.

New opportunities

Mozart lived at a time of great social change. While he took advantage of jobs that the church and courts offered, he also saw opportunities elsewhere that Leopold did not. At that time a rich middle class of merchants and traders was emerging. These people demanded music in the same way as the aristocracy did. They liked to dance, and they wanted to hear music from the latest Italian operas. They also wanted music that they could play at home. These demands influenced the type of music that composers wrote.

Concerts and recitals

Concerts as we know them hardly existed when Mozart was young. Public performances of music were a new idea when he visited Paris as a child. But by the time he returned there in 1778, concerts were very popular. Some of the musicians who performed at these concerts became extremely famous. Mozart himself became very well-known in this way.

A ticket for one of Mozart's concerts

A professional composer

Mozart played his own pieces at concerts, so he became famous not only as a performer but as a composer too. Many rich people paid him to compose pieces specially for them. For the first time, it became possible for him and others to earn a living writing music. Ever since Mozart's time composers have written for concert audiences, rather than the church or noblemen.

Mozart in 1790

Dancing became very popular in the 18th century.

Musical forms in Mozart's time

In the 18th century, many people in Europe became interested in the Ancient Greeks and Romans. They began to copy the neatness they saw in ancient art, and developed ordered, precise styles of painting, architecture and writing. For example, the formal garden was an 18th-century invention. Flowers and hedges were planted in complicated, detailed patterns. The idea was that people saw both the individual flowers and the larger shapes they made, and would find both beautiful and interesting.

In gardens like this, the individual plants and flowers make a larger pattern.

In the same way, the tunes in this book are beautiful and interesting. But each one also belongs to a larger piece, like a concerto or a symphony. If you listen to a recording of *Eine kleine Nachtmusik*, you will hear a longer piece than the one on page 47. You will hear the tune shown there, then several others.

A long piece with only one tune* would be boring. But one with many tunes might also be confusing. For a long piece to work well, the tunes must be combined in special ways. These combinations are known as the "form" of a piece. Mozart is a

In a row of 18th-century houses like this, the individual buildings make up a larger architectural form.

great composer because he wrote beautiful tunes and combined them into forms so skilfully.

Each piece of music has its own individual form. Parts may be played in different keys or by different instruments. The notes or rhythms of the themes may be changed. All these changes and contrasts make up the form of the piece.

In a string quartet (see pages 34-35), the themes often move from one instrument to another.

In a long piece, one obvious feature of its form is the way it is split into sections or movements. In Mozart's time, symphonies usually had four movements. Each one has its own themes, and may be faster, slower, louder or softer than the others.

Sonata form

When musicians in the 19th century heard pieces by Mozart and other composers of his time, they realized many individual movements had a similar form. Each one had its own themes, but they were combined in a similar way. (18th-century composers may not have known they were doing this. It probably seemed quite natural to them.) 19th-century musicians found this form in sonatas (pieces for one or two instruments), so they called it "sonata form". But they also saw it in other kinds of 18th-century music. The box below explains how sonata form works.

An early publication of sonatas by Mozart

How sonata form works

In a sonata-form movement, there are usually two themes at the start. They are in two different keys, such as C major and G major, or A minor and C major. The tunes are combined and altered in many elaborate ways. They are then repeated towards the end of the movement, this time in the same key. One reason why people admired pieces in sonata form so much was that they seemed to do two things at once. The tunes are heard clearly, then they are changed and broken up, and are put back together again at the end. Also, when the tunes are first heard, they are in different keys. When they reappear at the end they are in the same key, and so they seem to have moved together.

At the beginning, the first and second themes are in different keys.

In the middle, they are combined and altered in many different ways.

At the end, the two themes are heard in their original forms, but in the same key.

In a long piece of music, each tune is called a theme.

Divertimento, K113

A divertimento is usually a light-hearted piece in several movements. The word is Italian for an entertainment.

This was the first piece of Mozart's to use clarinets. He heard them first in Italy. They were not available in Salzburg.

14

Violin concerto in A, K219

As well as being a brilliant keyboard player, Mozart also played the violin and viola to a very high standard.

In 1775 he wrote four violin concertos to perform himself. This one is sometimes known as the Turkish concerto.

The violin

The greatest of all violin makers was Antonio Stradivari (known as Stradivarius). He lived in Cremona in northern Italy and died in 1737. He made over 1000 violins, of which about 650 survive.

Antonius Stradivarius Cremonensis
Faciebat Anno 1724

Stradivarius's trademark

Designs for a violin by Stradivarius

A court composer

By the end of 1773 Wolfgang's days touring as a child musician were over. He now had to compete with others for work. In 1771 he was given a part-time job in Salzburg at the archbishop's court, but the following year a new archbishop, Colloredo, was elected. He was less understanding, and did not like his musicians touring Europe trying to make their own fortunes. He believed that they were paid to provide his court with music, and he was unhappy to let them travel.

Colloredo did allow Leopold and Wolfgang to visit Munich, where Wolfgang had been asked to write a new opera, *La finta giardiniera* ("The pretend gardener"). But after returning to Salzburg, Wolfgang quickly became impatient with the restrictions of musical life there.

Leopold's home in Salzburg

Mozart and his father did not find their daily work at the court as interesting and enjoyable as their travels. Wolfgang spent his time teaching, playing in the court orchestra, and composing music for court occasions. But by 1777 he was frustrated and bored. He decided to return to Paris to look for work. He asked the archbishop to release him and Leopold from their court positions to travel once more.

Colloredo finally agreed, but in fact Leopold had to ask for his job back when he realized he could not afford to support the whole family. Only Wolfgang and his mother went to Paris. For the first time, he was parted from his father. Leopold's letters to Wolfgang show that he was unhappy because he no longer had as much control over his son's career.

First Wolfgang visited Munich. At the Nymphenburg Palace, where as children he and Nannerl had performed so successfully, he made himself unpopular by insulting the composers who worked there. In Augsburg, Leopold's birthplace, Wolfgang visited the Stein piano factory. He wrote to his father about the instruments, praising their beautiful tone.

The next stop was Mannheim. The court orchestra there was the finest in Europe. Though Mozart did not compose specifically for the orchestra, the effect of hearing it greatly increased his idea of what was possible in a symphony (see page 25).

An 18th-century painting of the city of Mannheim

Although he was not offered a job at the court in Mannheim, Mozart did take part in musical activities there for four months. He also taught the children of several court musicians. These included Rosina, the daughter of Christian Cannabich, the director of the orchestra.

Cannabich introduced Mozart to the Weber family. He fell in love with one of the daughters, Aloysia. Her mother was a very ambitious woman, and tried to persuade him to tour Italy with them and make their fortune.

A silhouette of Frau Weber

Aloysia Weber

When Wolfgang wrote to his father suggesting this, Leopold ordered his son to continue to Paris instead to find proper work. Wolfgang and his mother reached Paris in March 1778. At first the prospects seemed good. But Mozart felt that the people did not make him welcome, and they thought he was arrogant. They had little time for young, unknown composers.

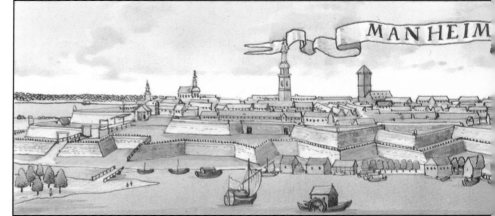

Mozart at the age of 11

Paris in the 18th century

There were some possibilities, however. Paris was one of the few European cities at the time to hold public concerts. For one of these Mozart wrote his symphony no.31, now known as the "Paris" symphony. He was also able to earn money from teaching. One of his pupils was the daughter of the Duc de Guines. The Duc was an excellent flautist and his daughter played the harp very well. Mozart composed for them the concerto for flute and harp, K299.

The manuscript of the opening of the "Paris" symphony

Back to Salzburg

In July 1778 Wolfgang's mother died after a short illness, and he was left alone in Paris. Leopold realized his son had no chance of finding work there. Distressed by his wife's death, he wanted Wolfgang to return to Salzburg. He persuaded Archbishop Colloredo to appoint Wolfgang as the court organist. Leopold wanted his son to have a better future than this, but knew that it was better than him having no work in Paris.

Wolfgang wanted to see his father again, but from his letters we know that he did not want to return to Salzburg. He went first to Munich, where the Webers now lived. But when he arrived there, he found that Aloysia no longer loved him. This made him even more unhappy. It took him over five months to reach home. Leopold was angry, thinking the archbishop would give the job of organist to someone else. But Wolfgang arrived in December and began work at the court.

For two years Mozart had to put up with a dull routine of teaching and playing. But late in 1780 he was asked to write an opera for a carnival in Munich. The piece he wrote, *Idomeneo*, was performed early the following year. It was quite successful, and this made Mozart even more impatient to leave the archbishop's court to seek work independently.

Mozart's mother, Maria Anna

Arguments with Colloredo

In March 1781, Joseph II was crowned emperor of Austria. Archbishop Colloredo went to Vienna for the celebrations, taking his court musicians with him. Mozart wrote angrily to his father about the conditions there.

The title page of *Idomeneo*

He complained that he was being treated as a servant, and made to sit with the kitchen staff. This offended his pride, as he was used to being treated as a celebrity, particularly after the success of his opera in Munich.

Mozart and the archbishop had many other disagreements. Most importantly, Mozart felt cheated because Colloredo would not allow him to make extra money by playing in public concerts. The two men lost patience with each other. After a fierce argument, Mozart was told to leave. As he went, he was kicked down the stairs by one of the archbishop's servants.

The Haffner serenade, K250

When he was 19, Mozart was asked to write this piece by Siegmund Haffner, a Salzburg businessman.

It was played at a celebration on the evening before the wedding of Haffner's sister, Marie Elisabeth.

Another serenade written for the Haffner family was later turned into the Haffner Symphony, K385.

Siegmund Haffner

The left hand has to play three eighth notes in the same time as one quarter note. These are called triplets.

The serenade

A serenade was originally a piece intended to be played in the evening, often outdoors. Although Mozart later turned a few of his serenades into symphonies, they were really intended as dance music.

Piano sonata, K309

Mozart wrote this piece in 1777, while he was staying at the court of Mannheim. This is part of the first movement.

The orchestra at Mannheim was famous for its dramatic fanfares. The opening of the piece imitates this style.

The piano

At the start of the 18th century, one of the most common keyboard instruments was the harpsichord. No matter how hard the keys of a harpsichord are hit, the sound is always the same. A little leather flap, or plectrum, plucks the strings, and the player can not adjust the volume.

In about 1700, in Florence, Italy, a man named Cristofori invented a keyboard instrument that could play both loud (*forte*) and soft (*piano*). In this instrument the strings are not plucked, but hit by small, felt-covered hammers. The harder

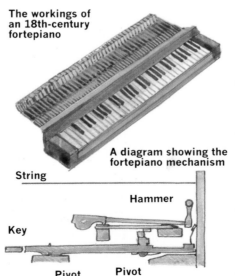

The workings of an 18th-century fortepiano

A diagram showing the fortepiano mechanism

String

Hammer

Key

Pivot   Pivot

the key is pressed, the harder the hammer hits the strings, and the louder the note sounds.

Cristofori called his instrument *gravicembalo con forte e piano* ("harpsichord with loud and soft"), which led to its early name "fortepiano". This later became "pianoforte", and eventually simply "piano". 18th century pianos are still often referred to as fortepianos.

Mozart wrote a lot of music to be played by amateurs, often in their own homes. As not everybody owned a piano, he marked it simply "for keyboard" without saying which sort.

This sonata was written for Rosina, the daughter of Christian Cannabich. Cannabich directed the orchestra at Mannheim.

The small notes at the start are called *acciaccatura* ("a-cha-ka-too-ra"), meaning "crushed". Play them as quickly as possible.

Mozart's sonatas

In all, Mozart wrote 32 keyboard sonatas, as well as others for violin and keyboard. Some, like this one, were written for his pupils. Others were much more difficult and were intended to display his own skills when he performed them at concerts.

Mozart's sonatas usually had three movements. Like this one, the first movement was lively, or as the music says, *con spirito* ("with spirit"). This was to attract the attention of the listeners.

You can find extracts of the second and third movements of this sonata on pages 22 and 23.

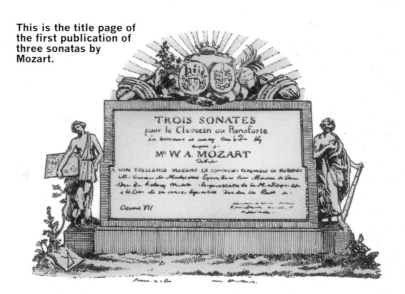

This is the title page of the first publication of three sonatas by Mozart.

Piano sonata, K309 (second movement)

It is said that this movement was a musical portrait of the 13 year-old Rosina Cannabich.

Adagio is Italian for "at ease". *Andante* means "moving" or "flowing". So, the tempo is "flowing, a little at ease".

Piano sonata, K309 (finale)

The final movement (sometimes just called the "finale") was usually fast.

Allegretto means quite fast, though slower than *allegro*. *Grazioso* means "gracefully".

The second movement

The second movement was often slow. It was sometimes marked *Andante*. This suggests a flowing, steady speed, such as would be suitable for dancing. The slow movement was often in a different key, to contrast with the first and third movements.

An 18th-century cartoon of a piano duet

The finale

Many finales had a pattern called a "rondo". This meant that a tune would return several times. The music would sound as though it was going off in a new direction, but it would return to the main tune each time.

The orchestra

In ancient Greece, the round space where plays were performed was called the orchestra, which means "dancing place". In the 17th century the word was used in French theaters for the part of the stage where musicians sat. By the 18th century the players themselves were known as the orchestra.

Orchestras in Mozart's time were different from the standard symphony orchestras of today. The number and type of instruments varied, according to what players were available and what type of music was being played. But most orchestras in Mozart's time followed a basic pattern and layout. This is described below.

Wind instruments

The wind section usually consisted of pairs of flutes, oboes, clarinets and bassoons, However not all 18th-century orchestras included all these instruments. In orchestras that were short of players, oboists often had to be able to play the flute or the clarinet as well. In Mozart's time most of these instruments were made of wood. Today most flutes are made of metal.

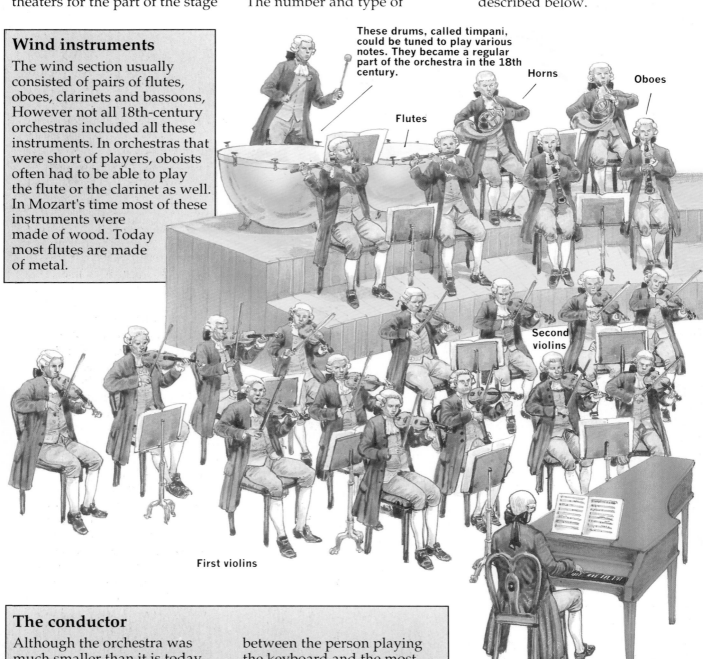

These drums, called timpani, could be tuned to play various notes. They became a regular part of the orchestra in the 18th century.

Horns

Oboes

Flutes

Second violins

First violins

The orchestra also included a keyboard, to reinforce the sound of the other instruments. In orchestral concerts this was usually a harpsichord.

The conductor

Although the orchestra was much smaller than it is today, it still had at least 25 players. The musicians needed a leader to keep them playing together. There was no separate conductor, as there is today. The conducting was shared between the person playing the keyboard and the most senior violinist. When Mozart played the solo part in his own piano concertos, he usually conducted the orchestra himself from his seat at the keyboard.

Brass

The brass section consisted of trumpets, trombones and horns. These instruments are made from lengths of brass tubing, curled round to make them easier to carry and play. 18th-century horns and trumpets had a more limited range of notes than violins, so they often had less to play in orchestral pieces. But because they could play loudly, they were used when the music reached a climax. Some brass instruments were only used for certain occasions. For example, trombones were normally only used for church music.

Mozart's orchestra today

During the 19th century the number of players in a standard orchestra grew to nearly a hundred. In addition, new inventions made instruments sound louder. Complicated keys were added to woodwind instruments to enable them to be played faster. Brass insruments were given valves, so that players did not have to carry so many crooks with them (see p.45).

These changes brought many improvements, but they also altered the sound of the orchestra. In recent years people have wondered how the music would have sounded in Mozart's time, before all these changes. Now there are many orchestras and groups using what are known as "original" or "authentic" instruments. These are either copies of instruments from the 18th century, or ones made at that time that have not been altered. The Orchestra of the Age of Enlightenment, the Academy of Ancient Music and the London Classical Players are three orchestras who use original instruments.

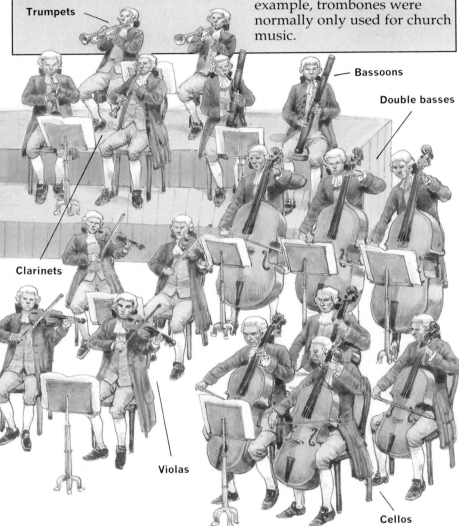

Trumpets

Bassoons

Double basses

Clarinets

Violas

Cellos

Stringed instruments

All orchestras had a group of stringed instruments: violins, violas, cellos and double basses. There were more violins than any other instrument, and they were divided into two groups. The number of violinists depended on the type of orchestra. A church orchestra had about 12 violinists, an opera house about 14. Orchestras for public concerts had about 19. In addition, there were usually around four violas, four cellos, and three double basses.

Concerto for flute and harp

This concerto was written for a French nobleman, the Comte de Guines, and his daughter.

The rhythm of this movement is that of a French dance, called the gavotte.

Allegro

Posthorn serenade, K320

Guards on mail coaches blew posthorns to announce their arrival. The posthorn was not usually used in orchestras.

In this serenade, Mozart included a section for a real posthorn. Today it is normally played by an orchestral horn.

Codes and puzzles

Mozart wrote letters to his father explaining his argument with Colloredo (see page 17). He suspected that the archbishop was reading them, so he used a cipher or code. He substituted some letters of the alphabet for others. For example, he exchanged M with A, L with E, O with S, F with I and H with U. So "Mozart's cipher" becomes *Aszmrt'o cfpulr*. He played other word games in his letters, often spelling his name backwards.

m e o f h
a e s i u

Mozart's   Aszmrt'o
cipher   cfpulr

trazom

27

After being dismissed from Salzburg by Archbishop Colloredo (see page 17), Mozart began teaching music in Vienna. He had several pupils, and taught them to compose and play the piano. One pupil was so good that he composed a sonata for two pianos to play with her.

Vienna in the 18th century

In Vienna he stayed with the Weber family (see page 16), who were living there at the time. Mozart had been in love with Aloysia Weber, but she had married someone else. Now news reached Leopold in Salzburg that Mozart was in love with her younger sister Constanze. In order to deny this, Mozart moved out of the Webers' house, insisting to his father that he did not want to marry Constanze.

Mozart at the age of 26

At this time, Mozart was asked to write a new opera based on a Turkish story. The opera, known as *Il seraglio*, quickly became one of his most popular pieces.

Mozart finally admitted to his father that he was in love with Constanze, and asked his permission to marry her. But Leopold did not trust her family, thinking that her mother had tricked Wolfgang into marrying

Constanze Weber

Constanze. When Wolfgang convinced his father that this was not true, Leopold agreed to the marriage. In August 1782, a few days after the first performance of *Il seraglio*, Wolfgang and Constanze married at St Stephen's Cathedral.

St Stephen's Cathedral, Vienna

Above right: the marriage certificate of Wolfgang and Constanze

Mozart was making a good living in Vienna from teaching, composing and giving concerts. But he and Constanze soon had troubles with money. After they were married they did not visit Leopold in Salzburg for almost a year, so that Mozart could continue to earn money teaching and performing. By the time they went they had had their first baby. As long journeys were difficult in those days, particularly with small

The Mozarts' apartment in Vienna

children, they left their son with a nurse in Vienna. When they returned, he had died. Though Constanze later had five more children, only two of them survived (see page 56).

Mozart's career in Vienna settled down to a comfortable routine of teaching, performing and having music published. When Leopold visited Wolfgang and Constanze in 1785, he found them living in a beautiful apartment, with a carriage and servants. It seemed to prove to Leopold that Wolfgang had become very successful after all.

Mozart composed six string quartets dedicated to Joseph Haydn, the composer he most admired (see page 35). Haydn was at the first performance, and told Leopold that Mozart was the greatest composer who had ever lived.

At the end of 1785, Mozart began composing an opera to words by Lorenzo da Ponte (see page 41). Da Ponte wrote the words for three of Mozart's best-known operas. The first of these was *The Marriage of Figaro*, which was based on a play by the writer Beaumarchais. Mozart composed the opera in a few months at the end of 1785 but it was not performed until May 1786.

At that time there were many rivalries among composers in Vienna. They all wanted to be chosen for the most important work, so they tried to outwit

A scene from *The Marriage of Figaro*

each other to gain positions of advantage. One such composer at the imperial court was Antonio Salieri. He may have been responsible for the delays in having *The Marriage of Figaro* performed. Mozart later accused Salieri of trying to poison him, perhaps because he was bitter about the delay. The opera was finally shown at the Burgtheater in Vienna, and then at many other opera houses in Germany. When it was later performed in Prague, the theater manager

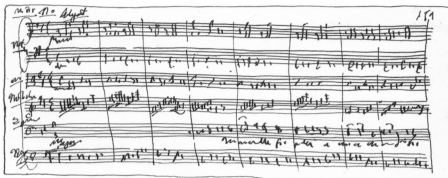

The first movement of Mozart's Requiem

Salieri

was so impressed that he asked Mozart to write another opera.

Before the new opera was finished, Leopold died. But even this tragedy did not stop Mozart from composing. The next opera, *Don Giovanni*, was finished only two days before it was first performed in Prague. It was another great success, making Mozart one of the most famous composers in Vienna. But in spite of this achievement, he and his wife continued to have serious financial troubles.

A scene from *Don Giovanni* (see page 50)

From this time until his death, Mozart often had to write letters to friends asking them for money. Both he and Constanze were often ill. Medicines were expensive, and illness stopped him working. Even so, by the start of 1790 he had written a third opera with Da Ponte, *Così fan tutte*. He was also working with a different librettist on another one, *The Magic Flute*.

In the summer of 1791, Mozart was visited by

Papageno the birdcatcher from The Magic Flute

a man he described as "an unknown, grey messenger". The stranger was in fact a servant of a local nobleman, Count Walsegg Stuppach. The Count's wife had died, and he wanted Mozart to write a requiem (a piece of funeral music). People have discussed ever since the possibility that Mozart thought the requiem was for himself. While writing it he became increasingly ill, and it was never finished. By November 1791, fever had made him unable to leave his bed. He died on December 5.

At that time many people feared they might be buried alive, so the authorities always waited for two days before a burial. Mozart was buried on December 7.

The house in Vienna where Mozart died

As was usual at the time, his body was placed in a communal grave outside the city, and his grave was not marked in any way. However a memorial to him has since been built in Vienna, and the entire city of Salzburg has become a memorial to Mozart's life.

The memorial to Mozart in Vienna

Serenade for wind instruments, K361

This serenade is known as the *Gran Partita* ("grand suite"). It is for twelve wind instruments and double bass.

Part of it may have been composed as a wedding present from Mozart to his wife, and played at their wedding dinner.

Wind bands

Groups of wind instruments, known in German as *Harmonie*, were mainly popular with the army and in country taverns. Then in 1782 Joseph II, the Emperor in Vienna, decided to employ a *Harmonie*. Until that time most music at court had been played by string instruments. However Joseph II wanted a wind band to play arrangements of operas at royal concerts, and to provide background music at mealtimes.

Wind bands (see below) were most popular around Vienna. In Italy, music for strings was more common.

When he first heard the sound of wind bands Mozart was very excited. It changed his ideas about writing for the orchestra.

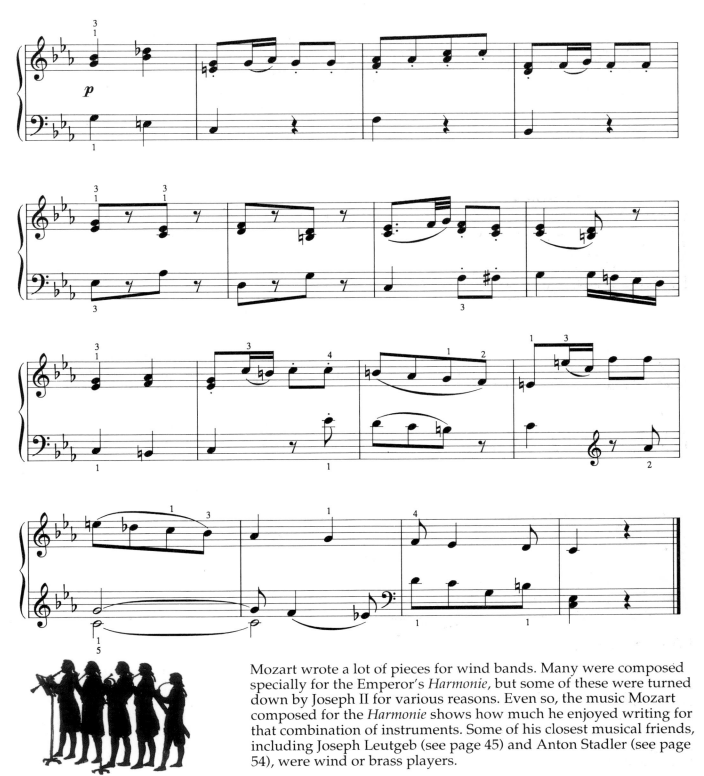

Mozart wrote a lot of pieces for wind bands. Many were composed specially for the Emperor's *Harmonie*, but some of these were turned down by Joseph II for various reasons. Even so, the music Mozart composed for the *Harmonie* shows how much he enjoyed writing for that combination of instruments. Some of his closest musical friends, including Joseph Leutgeb (see page 45) and Anton Stadler (see page 54), were wind or brass players.

Sinfonia concertante, K364

A sinfonia concertante is a sort of lighthearted concerto for more than one solo instrument. In this piece the soloists play violin and viola.

Viola

Violin

E♭ was a difficult key for viola players. Usually they had to tune the viola up a semitone and play as if the piece were in D. This retuning is known as *scordatura*.

Concerts

When he first went to Vienna, Mozart made most of his money by performing in public concerts. Most concerts were a lot longer than modern ones. They usually included an orchestra, which played one or two symphonies. Sometimes the symphonies were split up, so that only the first two or three movements were played at the beginning of the concert. The rest were performed at the end.

After the symphonies there were either a number of operatic arias (see page 8) or other vocal pieces. They were sung by members of the Italian opera company that worked in Vienna.

The Augarten,
a park in Vienna
where concerts were held

Then there was usually a concerto. In his own keyboard concertos, Mozart himself usually played the solo part. After this he entertained the audience by improvising (making music up on the spot). To do this he took a popular theme, or one from a symphony or aria, and made up variations on it. Mozart enjoyed making the improvisation as difficult as possible, to show off his skill. This was often the most popular part of the concert.

The orchestra would then join the composer for a grand finish, usually the fast and exciting final movement of a symphony.

This is the last movement of the piece. It should be played very quickly and lightly. Practice it slowly at first, then gradually build up speed.

Try to make a clear contrast between the short repeated notes, like those in the first three bars, and the smooth phrases like those in bars 4, 5 and 6.

Arranging

As public concerts became more and more popular, the audiences began to take an interest in all aspects of music. They wanted to read and learn about it, but most importantly, they wanted to play it themselves at home. They often wanted to play the pieces they heard at concerts. Of course they could not perform concertos or symphonies at home, because those works needed many players. But it was possible for someone to rewrite the pieces, so that they could be played on the piano (as with the pieces in this book) or by a string quartet. This is known as making an arrangement of a piece.

A 18th-century picture of people making music at home.

Today, if you want to make an arrangement of a piece of music by a composer who is still alive, you have to ask his or her permission. In the 18th century, however, the law was different. Anybody was allowed to make a new version of a composer's music and sell it through a publisher. Many arrangers made money this way because there was such a growing demand for music. Leopold often told Mozart to arrange his pieces quickly so that he would get the profit before someone else did.

String quartet, K465 (part B)

This is part of a string quartet (see below) arranged for two people playing the same piano. The person playing part B sits on the left.

In a quartet, the music on this page would be played by the viola and the cello. The music on the right would be played by the two violins.

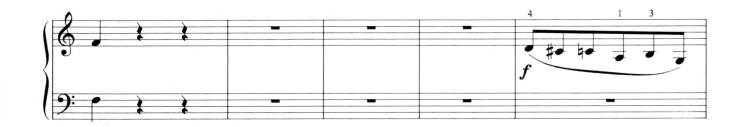

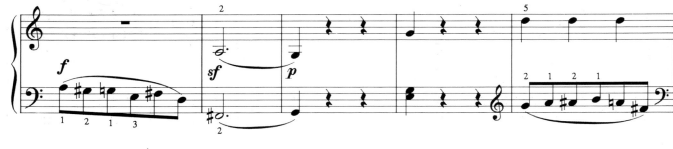

String quartets

Today the string quartet (two violins, a viola and a cello) is a very popular combination of instruments. Many composers have written music specially for it. The quartet developed in the 18th century. It is likely that it began because people wanted to play symphonies at home. They could not assemble a whole orchestra, but it was possible to make arrangements of orchestral pieces so that they could be played by four individual players.

Violins   Viola   Cello

String quartet, K465 (part A)

This was one of six quartets that Mozart dedicated to his friend, the composer Joseph Haydn, shown here.

At the first performance, Haydn told Leopold "Your son is the greatest composer known to me by name or in person".

In the 18th-century, violin and viola players stood up to play.

Mozart played in a string quartet with three of the most famous composers of his time: Haydn, Johann Vanhal and Carl von Dittersdorff. Haydn was the first composer to write quartets that were not simply arrangements or imitations of orchestral music. His pieces took advantage of the special sound qualities produced by four single stringed instruments. This idea inspired Mozart to write his own string quartets, with the same sound quality in mind.

from Duos for horns, K487

Mozart wrote these duos (pieces for two players) in 1786. They may have been a gift for a friend, probably Joseph Leutgeb (see page 44).

He did not say for which instruments they were written; it was either two french horns (shown here) or two basset horns (see below).

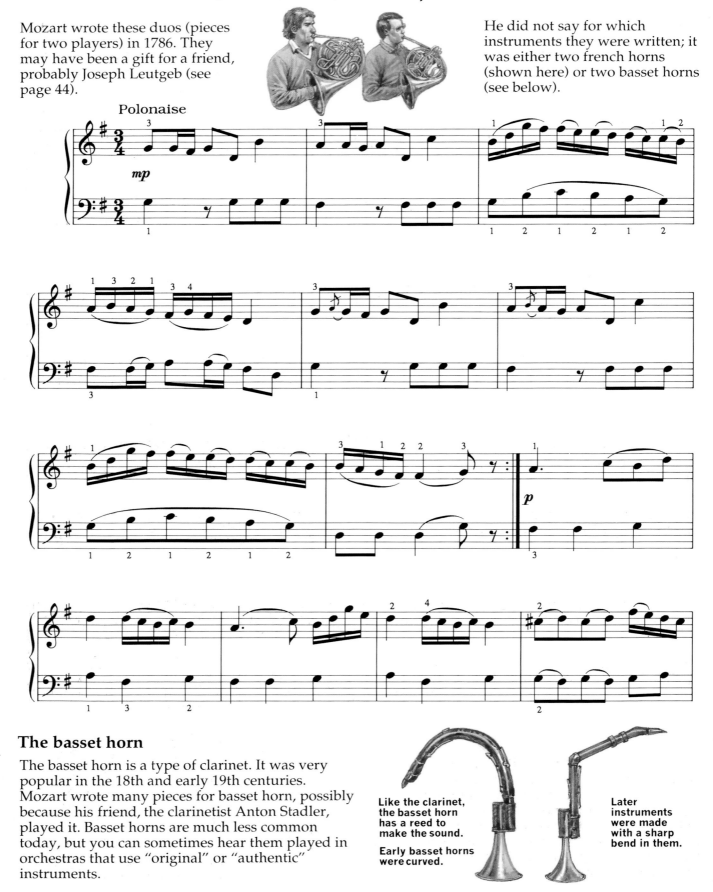

The basset horn

The basset horn is a type of clarinet. It was very popular in the 18th and early 19th centuries. Mozart wrote many pieces for basset horn, possibly because his friend, the clarinetist Anton Stadler, played it. Basset horns are much less common today, but you can sometimes hear them played in orchestras that use "original" or "authentic" instruments.

Like the clarinet, the basset horn has a reed to make the sound.

Early basset horns were curved.

Later instruments were made with a sharp bend in them.

This piece is based on a type of dance called the Polonaise. You can find out more about this below.

You could play the top line of this piece on the violin, flute or recorder. Ask a friend to play the bottom line on the piano or cello.

The Polonaise

The Polonaise developed in Poland, probably in the 16th century, and was popular all over Europe for hundreds of years. Because it was formal and dignified, it was often danced at weddings and public ceremonies. Music for the Polonaise is slow and stately, usually in three-four time. The dancers take a long, steady step on each beat of the bar. Try not to rush this piece when you play it.

The Polonaise is danced by many pairs of dancers, in a long procession.

37

from Duos for horns, K487

This piece is from the same set of twelve duos as the Polonaise on pages 36-37.

To improve basset horns, people built them in different shapes. This one has a rounded bell and a special key mechanism.

Larghetto

Ludwig von Köchel

Mozart's pieces are usually identified by "K" or "Köchel" numbers. These are named after Ludwig von Köchel ("ker-shel"), an Austrian geologist and botanist (1800-1877). He compiled an index of all the works of Mozart that were known to exist, as well as those thought to have been lost. His catalogue has been revised and corrected several times since then, as more has been discovered about Mozart's life. Many pieces are known mainly by the numbers Köchel gave them.

Piano concerto in A, K488

Unlike many later composers, Mozart did not include many indications of loud and soft in his piano music.

But he did show carefully which notes should be slurred together and which should be played separately, or staccato.

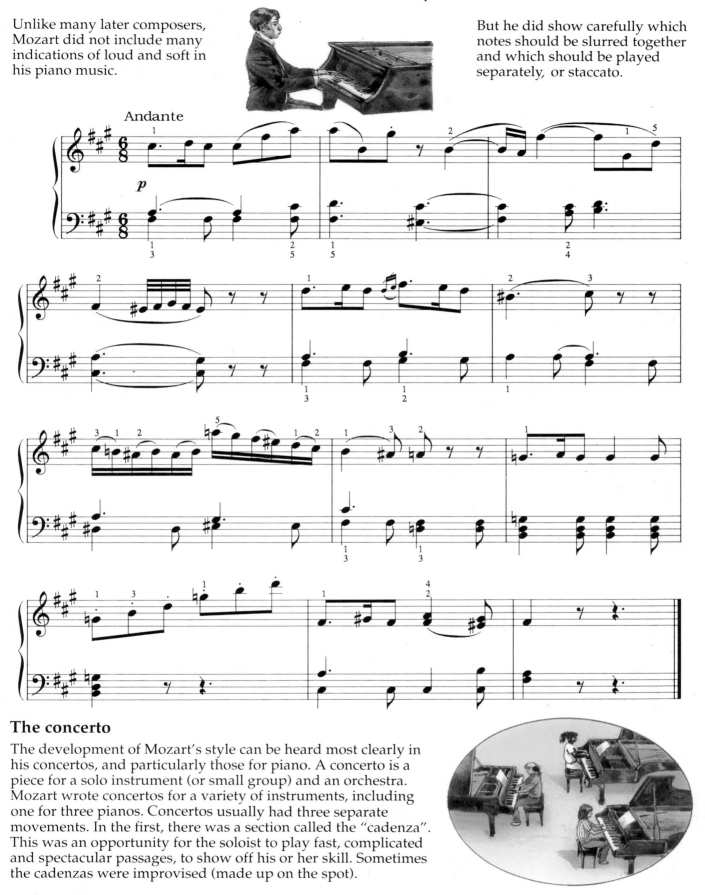

The concerto

The development of Mozart's style can be heard most clearly in his concertos, and particularly those for piano. A concerto is a piece for a solo instrument (or small group) and an orchestra. Mozart wrote concertos for a variety of instruments, including one for three pianos. Concertos usually had three separate movements. In the first, there was a section called the "cadenza". This was an opportunity for the soloist to play fast, complicated and spectacular passages, to show off his or her skill. Sometimes the cadenzas were improvised (made up on the spot).

Opera

At the end of the 16th century, a group of Italian scholars developed a new way of combining words and music. They used this for a new form of musical drama which became known as opera. By the time Mozart went to Italy in 1770, opera was the most popular type of music there, and there were opera houses (special theaters for opera) all over Europe. Opera is still a very popular form of entertainment, and Mozart's operas are some of the most famous.

Operas are like plays, except that most of the words are sung. They are performed with scenery, which is often moved by complicated machinery. The singers perform in costumes, and are usually accompanied by an orchestra.

The stage machinery below created the effect of a ship at sea

Machinery for changing scenery

Opera houses were opened all over Europe. This one was built in Vienna, Austria, in the 19th century.

In Mozart's time there were three main types of opera: *singspiel*, *opera seria* and *opera buffa*. Mozart wrote several of each. In addition he wrote other theatrical pieces that we now would not think of as operas. Some had spoken parts, and others contained ballet dances.

Singspiel

Singspiel is German for "song-play". It was the most popular style of opera in Germany. The stories were usually light-hearted comedies, and included spoken words as well as songs. Mozart wrote five singspiels. The most famous are *The Magic Flute* (see pages 58-59) and *Il seraglio.*

19th-century stage design for *The Magic Flute*

Opera seria

Opera seria is Italian for "serious opera". All the words are sung, so there are no spoken parts. Most of the stories are from ancient history and mythology.

A scene from an *opera seria*

The characters were mainly gods and goddesses or kings and queens. The stories always had a happy ending in which the hero was rewarded for good deeds and the villain was punished for bad ones. Mozart's most important operas in this style are *Lucio Silla* (see page 10) and *La Clemenza di Tito.*

Words and music

The words of an opera are called the libretto (Italian for "little book"), and the writer is called the librettist. The words were usually written before the music. Mozart's most famous librettists were Emanuel Schikaneder and Lorenzo da Ponte.

Schikaneder was an actor, singer, and theater manager, as well as a librettist. He even wrote music for two of his own libretti. For Mozart, he wrote the words to *The Magic Flute*. He also appeared in its first performance as Papageno the bird-catcher, and owned the theater where the first performance took place.

Emanuel Schikaneder

Da Ponte was an Italian priest, but he was forced to leave Venice after he was involved in a scandal. In 1779 he went to Vienna, where he became the resident librettist for the Italian opera company. Three of Mozart's operas have words by Da Ponte: *The Marriage of Figaro*, *Don Giovanni*, and *Così fan Tutti*.

Lorenzo da Ponte

Opera buffa

Opera buffa (comic opera) was rather different from the other types. The characters were real people, not gods and goddesses, and the plots were based on events that happen in real life. The stories included both happy and sad moments, and everybody was shown to have good points and bad ones. For example, in *The Marriage of Figaro*, Mozart's most famous *opera buffa*, the characters include a Count and Countess and their servants. The story describes the various misunderstandings and confusions that happen during the preparations for a wedding.

Singing stars

The stars of the operas were the singers, not the composers. The best ones were paid huge amounts of money for their performances, and were adored by their fans. The most important singers were the sopranos (women with the highest voices) and the castratos (men whose voices had never broken). The sopranos were usually given the most spectacular pieces (called arias). The Queen of the Night's aria on page 58 is a good example.

Nancy Storace, a famous 18th-century singer

The singers had so much power and influence that composers often wrote new arias for them to sing during another composer's opera. These pieces are called "insert arias", and they often had nothing to do with the story. They were only there to show off the singer's skill.

The opening of *The Marriage of Figaro*

Symphony no.34 in C

This symphony was written in Salzburg. It was played in 1782 at a concert in a pavilion in the Augarten, a park in Vienna (shown here).

It was the first of Mozart's symphonies to be played in Vienna, though he had been composing them since he was ten years old.

The symphony

A symphony is a large piece of music for orchestra. The idea developed from the *sinfonia*, the piece used in Italy to introduce an opera. By the 18th century the sinfonia had a fixed form of three sections or movements: fast, slow, fast.

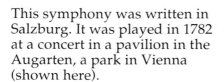

Trumpets were used in opera overtures to attract the audience's attention. This idea was transferred to the symphony as well.

The sinfonia became popular with concert audiences outside Italy. German composers often copied its form, but they added an extra movement, based on the minuet (see page 48). This later became the standard form of the symphony.

Dove sono

This is an aria from *The Marriage of Figaro*, one of Mozart's most famous operas. It is a sad song sung by the Countess, one of the main characters.

Marcellina   **The Count**   **The Countess**
Silhouettes of the singers who played these characters at the first performance of the opera

The top line can be played on the flute, recorder or violin. Or you can play the top and bottom lines on the piano alone.

Horn concerto in E flat

Mozart notated the score of this piece in four different colours. Nobody is sure why he did this.

Some people think that it was just for fun, others think it shows different sorts of loud and soft .

The horn

The pieces Mozart wrote for the horn were for a very different instrument from the one we know today. It was simply a coiled brass tube with a flared end or "bell". The tube could only produce certain notes, and only in one key at a time. To play in different keys, players had to change the length of the horn by inserting or removing sections of tubing called crooks. Today, most horns have special parts called valves. By pressing the valves, players can open and close sections of tubing, and change to all keys without using crooks.

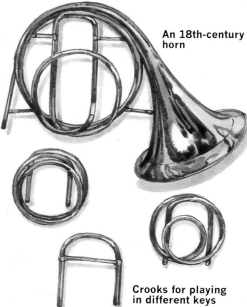

An 18th-century horn

Crooks for playing in different keys

In the 18th century, before the valved horn was invented, some players learned how to increase the number of notes they could play with one crook. They did this by placing their right hand inside the bell. This made the pitch lower, and altered the sound, making it quieter. It was very difficult to do this quickly and smoothly, but some players became especially good at it. One of these was Joseph Leutgeb (see opposite). Mozart made full use of Leutgeb's skills in his pieces, writing parts that demanded these new techniques.

Like almost all Mozart's works for horn, this concerto was written for Joseph Leutgeb (see below).

A modern horn player using a "natural" horn (one without valves).

Although it is known as number 4, it was actually the second of the four concertos he wrote for Leutgeb.

Joseph Leutgeb

The horn player Joseph Leutgeb was a friend of the Mozart family for the whole of Wolfgang's life. He played in the court orchestra in Salzburg with Leopold and Wolfgang. Leopold loaned him money when he moved to a suburb of Vienna in 1777 to open a shop. During the last years of Mozart's life, he and Leutgeb became firm friends. Mozart inserted jokes and insults into pieces he wrote for Leutgeb. One concerto reads "Wolfgang Amadé Mozart has taken pity on Leutgeb, ass, ox and fool, in Vienna on 27 May 1783."

Horn players need strong lips and teeth to control the sound of the instrument. But the pressure of playing can damage the teeth. Today, doctors and dentists know how to prevent this, but in Mozart's time they did not. This is why most horn players in those days were not full-time musicians. They needed another job, for when they became unable to play.

As Leutgeb grew older, he lost the ability to play very high or very low notes. In the last two concertos Mozart avoided writing notes that he knew Leutgeb could no longer play.

A musical joke

This piece was completed only two weeks after Leopold died. It makes fun of bad composers and players. Mozart's father liked this kind of joke.

It was written for two horns and a string quartet. This cartoon was on the front cover of the first publication.

46

Eine kleine Nachtmusik

The title is German for "a little night music", meaning a serenade (see page 19). This is part of the first movement.

The piece was written in 1787. This is how Mozart wrote down the opening of the piece in his catalogue (see page 52).

Eine kleine Nachtmusik (third movement)

Minuetto is Italian for "minuet", a type of French dance (see below). At this time, France was the most important country in Europe for style and fashion.

As well as copying French dances, the Viennese imitated French clothes. The ones shown here are Viennese versions of Parisian fashions of the 1780s.

Minuetto

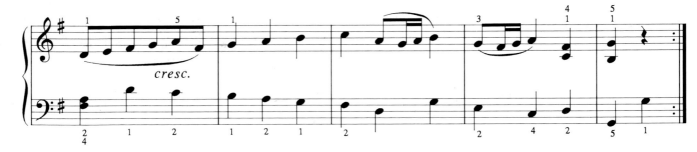

The minuet

The minuet was originally from France. By Mozart's time, however, it was the most popular dance with the aristocracy throughout Europe. It was a formal dance (one with strict steps and movements). It was apparently enjoyed as much by the people watching as by the dancers themselves. In a minuet the dancing couples weave around the dance floor in an S-shape.

A minuet has three beats to a bar. It is in two parts - the minuet itself and a contrasting section called the trio.

At first the trio was for three instruments, but later the word was applied to the second part of any minuet.

Trio

Although it started as a strict type of dance, the minuet quickly developed as a musical form of its own, and composers adapted it to their own styles. They started to put minuet sections into other pieces, such as string quartets and symphonies. Eventually minuets like this became too elaborate for dancing, but the minuet remained an important musical form for many years.

Là ci darem la mano

This is a duet from the opera *Don Giovanni*, which was first performed in 1787 at the National Theatre in Prague (shown here).

The opera is based on *The Playboy of Seville and the Stone Guest*, a story by the Spanish author Tirso de Molina.

Don Giovanni

Don Giovanni is an evil nobleman who takes advantage of everyone around him. Eventually he is punished when a man he has murdered comes back to life and drags him down to hell. *Don* is Italian for "lord".

The story of Don Giovanni has been used in many different ways. It is the basis of several other operas, and of poems, plays and novels by the writers Byron, Molière, Balzac and George Bernard Shaw.

from Adagio and rondo for glass harmonica

The glass harmonica is a box that contains glass bowls. The player presses a foot pedal to make the bowls revolve in a trough of water.

The player rubs his fingers against the bowls as they spin. This makes a strange sound, rather like a flute. Each bowl produces a different note.

Today, very few people play the glass harmonica. But you can hear the noise it made if you dip a glass in some water, then gently rub your finger round the rim. You may need to try several different glasses to make this work. Be very careful not to press too hard, or the glass might break.

Divertimento for string trio, K563

This is part of a piece for string trio (a violin, a viola and a cello). Here is the entry Mozart made for it in his thematic catalogue (see below).

At this time Mozart and Constanze were living in the Schulerstrasse in Vienna. On the opposite page is the room in which he probably worked.

Allegretto

Mozart's catalogue

In 1784 Mozart began compiling a catalogue of all the pieces he was writing. He wrote on the first page: "List of all my works from the month of February 1784 to the month ____ 1___". This shows that he probably thought he would live until at least 1800.

The catalogue listed the titles of his pieces, saying when they were written and for which instruments. By each title, Mozart wrote the first few bars of the first movement of the piece, like the one shown above. However, this list is not the most accurate catalogue of Mozart's music. It leaves out all the music he wrote before 1784. In addition, Mozart was writing so much music that he often lost track of it all. And in many cases, the descriptions have puzzled later experts because they do not provide enough information.

A page from Mozart's catalogue. The titles and details are on the left; the opening bars of each piece are on the right.

Although Mozart was well paid in Vienna, he and Constanze were often ill. This stopped him from composing, which meant he lost money.

When this happened he often had to borrow money from friends. One of them was Johann Puchberg, to whom this piece was dedicated.

Mozart and money

In the 1780s, living in Vienna was very expensive. Mozart had several ways of making money, but they all had disadvantages. He gave piano and composition lessons. These paid quite well, but took him away from his composing. He gave concerts, both in public and at the homes of noblemen, but from around 1783 he became less popular as a performer. He was paid for composing and for arranging pieces for people to play at home. But to be paid well for this sort of work he had to meet rich people. This was expensive,

because it meant going to the most fashionable places or holding parties and banquets.

In 1787, he was given a position at the imperial court in Vienna. This did not pay very well, but it was a more reliable way of earning a living than teaching or performing.

It has often been said that Mozart lived and died in poverty. In fact, by the standards of his time, he was not poor. But he never had a steady income that he could rely on.

This is one of the last portraits of Mozart. It was painted in 1789.

Clarinet quintet

Mozart's two greatest works for the clarinet, the Quintet and the Concerto, were written for his friend, Anton Stadler, shown here.

Stadler asked a Viennese instrument maker, Theodore Lotz, to build him a special clarinet, the basset clarinet (see below).

Larghetto

Mozart wrote for two types of clarinet that are today considered rather strange: the basset horn (see page 37) and the basset clarinet.

An 18th-century basset clarinet

The basset clarinet is not curved or bent like a basset horn. It is more like an ordinary clarinet, but slightly longer, enabling it to play lower notes.

54

The quintet is written for clarinet and string quartet. Stadler was a clarinetist in the court orchestra in Vienna.

The top line can be played on the flute, recorder or violin. Or play the top and bottom lines on the piano alone.

The basset clarinet was forgotten by composers and players in the 19th and early 20th centuries. But some modern musicians have begun using it again.

A modern basset clarinet

A few modern composers have written music for the basset clarinet, because of its special sound. The best known piece is *Linoi* by Harrison Birtwistle.

Ave verum corpus

This piece was written for the church at the town of Baden. The water that came from the hot springs there was believed to cure people's illnesses.

Mozart's wife Constanze went to Baden several times when she was ill. After she was cured, Mozart composed this piece to be played there.

Constanze Mozart

Constanze was six years younger than Mozart. Her father was a violinist and singer, and he had four daughters. Two became professional singers, and two married composers.

From his letters to Mozart, it seems that Leopold did not like Constanze very much. He thought she would distract Mozart from composing. However this was not the case, for after marrying Constanze Mozart wrote a huge amount of music.

Wolfgang and Constanze had six children, but only two lived beyond childhood. The younger of them, Franz Xaver, also became a composer.

After Mozart's death, Constanze married Georg Nissen, a Danish diplomat. With her help, he wrote the first biography of Mozart. When Nissen died, Constanze returned to Salzburg. She lived to the age of 80, and died in 1842.

Mozart's children Franz Xaver (left) and Karl Thomas

Constanze Mozart

Mozart spent much of his early career as a church musician in the cathedral in Salzburg.

His duties there included training the church choir and orchestra, and writing music for church services.

Church music

Mozart's first permanent job was at the cathedral in Salzburg. While he was there he wrote sixteen masses (pieces of music to accompany the main religious services). He continued writing church music even after he finally left Salzburg in 1781. At the time of his death, he was working on a Requiem (a funeral mass) for choir and orchestra.

Many bishops were worried about the use of new music in church. They claimed that performances had become more like concerts than church services. Large orchestras would play concertos and even accompany singers in operatic arias. As a result, many people began coming to church for the musical spectacle rather than for the services. Because of this, the bishops insisted that composers wrote less elaborate music. Eventually they stopped full orchestras playing in church.

This is the opening of the piece Mozart left incomplete when he died - the "Lachrymosa" from his Requiem (Mass for the dead).

Queen of the Night's aria

This aria is called "You will avenge me, daughter". It is from the opera *The Magic Flute*, which is set in ancient Egypt.

Constanze Mozart's eldest sister, Josepha Hofer, sang the role of the Queen of the Night at the first performances.

In the opera the Queen of the Night's daughter has been imprisoned in the palace of Sarastro, the Priest of the Sun.

Although Sarastro at first seems to be the villain, by the end it is clear that the Queen of the Night is the wicked one.

Sarastro's palace

Mozart in the future

The American spacecraft *Voyager 2* was launched in 1977. First it visited the outer planets of the solar system, then it continued its journey to explore deep space. In case it comes into contact with intelligent life, it contains various objects to provide information about human beings. One item is a video disc of a performance of the Queen of the Night's aria. There is no air in space, so nothing decays. Unless it crashes, *Voyager 2* will last for billions of years with Mozart's music on board.

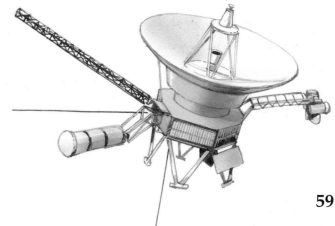

Playing the pieces

Below you will find some notes about playing the pieces in this book. They explain any difficult sections in the music, and give hints on how to practice and perform. The pieces appear in the book in the order Mozart wrote them. While this is not strictly in order of their difficulty, the pieces mostly get harder as you go through the book. But if you want to begin with the simplest pieces of all, look at the Violin concerto on page 15 and the Posthorn serenade on page 27.

To Mozart, it was more important to play music clearly than to play it quickly. Practice the most difficult bars in each piece until you can play them well, without worrying about the speed. When you can play smoothly, you can then play more quickly if needed. If it helps, practice each hand separately at first.

Mozart was very careful about how notes should be played together in groups, and whether they should be played staccato or legato. So you should always pay attention to slurs and phrase marks.

Gallimathias musicum

Allegretto means fairly fast. It also suggests that the piece should be played fairly lightly. First practice the sixteenth note passages. When you can play those smoothly, try the whole piece.

Senti l'eco

If you are playing this as a duet, you will need to agree on a speed. Count a few bars before you start. In the first eight bars, the top line should be a little louder than the accompaniment. From bar 9, the right hand of the piano takes the tune and the top line is then the echo.

from Lucio Silla

Make sure that the accompaniment in the first three bars is quiet. This will allow the tied note in the right hand to be heard for its full length.

Divertimento, K113

The sixteenth note scales in the last bars should be slightly more separated than a normal legato, but not played staccato.

Violin concerto, K219

Menuetto is Italian for "minuet", a kind of dance. You do not need to play quickly to make the piece sound like a dance, but you should make the third beat of each bar fairly light.

The Haffner serenade, K250

For most of this piece, the left hand plays in the treble clef. Practice the arpeggios (broken chords) so that you can play them staccato. You may find the rhythm of the first few bars difficult. Practice with a metronome until you can play the triplets and sixteenth notes exactly on the beat.

Piano sonata, K309

first movement: Practice the sixteenth notes near the end until you can play them smoothly and evenly.

second movement: Play this piece very lightly and delicately. Although the beat is slow, some of the notes are rather fast. However, you should be careful not to rush them.

finale: Make sure you can play the arpeggios (broken chords) in the left hand lightly and evenly. When you play the right hand line, make a contrast between the pairs of notes that are slurred and those that are not. (Lift your finger off the first note of each slurred pair a fraction of a second after you have struck the second one.) The ideal speed for this movement is about 110 beats per minute.

Concerto for flute and harp

The time signature means you should count only two fairly slow half note beats in each bar. Mozart notated exactly which notes should be played staccato and which legato. Make sure you play the repeated notes in the second half evenly.

Posthorn serenade, K320

Pay special attention to the fingerings in bars 6 and 9, where you must change finger during the rocking figure. Practice the beginning of bar 4 so that both hands play exactly together.

Serenade for wind instruments, K361

To imitate the sound of wind instruments, you have to make a very clear difference between staccato and legato. The top line of page 31 is fairly difficult. Try it a few times until you can play it evenly.

Sinfonia concertante, K364

Presto is very fast, about 170 beats per minute. But the piece is marked to be played quietly, so you should begin by playing it much more slowly. You must develop control of your fingers if you want to play fast but quietly.

String quartet, K465

To play duets, you have to know your own part well to be able to play with the other person. It may help if you each practice your parts separately at first, and try to memorize them. The first few times you play, count steadily all the way through so that you stay together. It is very important to listen to the other player's part as well as your own. (Listen for the echo effects in bars 5, 6 and 7.)

There are different difficulties in each part. Player A has to cross hands in the ninth bar, and needs finger control in the last 5 bars. In bars 4 and 5, player B has to play the right- and left-hand parts exactly together.

from Duos for horns, K487

In the Polonaise, the first horn (the right hand) is more important than the second (the left hand). Practice the right hand on its own first, paying special attention to the slurs. The speed should be between 80 and 90 beats per minute.

In the Larghetto the two parts are more equal. There are two slow beats to the bar, no faster than about 60 per minute.

Piano concerto, K488

The rhythm of the right hand at the beginning is the hardest thing about this piece. (A metronome may help.) In bars 2 and 3 the first notes of the main beats of the bar are not sounded, so keep the beat firmly in your mind all the time. Follow the fingerings for the left hand very carefully. Play delicately and gently, at an eighth note speed of about 110 beats per minute.

Symphony no.34 in C

Make sure the two-note chords do not sound too heavy, by touching the keys only very lightly.

Dove sono

The leaps in the left hand may need practice before you accompany a melody instrument. Count one or two bars before you begin. The broken line between the staffs at bar 16 tells you to play the E with your right hand.

Horn concerto in E flat

The left hand chords should be strong enough to give a clear bass line, but they should not intrude. In bar 8 the repeated notes in the left hand should be as loud as the right hand, because they continue the melody.

A musical joke

Orchestras usually play this piece at more than 200 beats per minute. This is difficult on the piano, but if you keep your wrists loose while you play, you will gradually pick up speed.

Eine kleine Nachtmusik

first movement: Make the opening very bold and confident. The second line should be gentler, with very light chords in the left hand.

third movement: The notes of this piece are fairly easy, so concentrate on how you touch the keyboard. Bars with three quarter notes, like bars 1 and 3, should be played with a slight separation between the notes, but hold the half note in bar 2 for its full length. The left-hand quarter notes should be smoother and softer. In the Trio, the right hand should be as smooth as possible, with the left hand a little louder and slightly staccato.

Là ci darem la mano

The left hand is not as easy as the tune here. Practice the leaps in bars 6, 10 and 11.

Adagio and rondo for glass harmonica

The top staff may be played on a recorder, flute or violin. Although the opening bars of both parts are marked *forte*, the melody instrument is most important. The rhythm of the melody is fairly difficult, so try not to play too quickly.

Divertimento for string trio, K563

The speed should be of a rather fast dance, about 150 beats per minute. At this speed the eighth notes will sound like staccatos. But do not play too quickly, or you will lose the contrast between the grace notes in bars 15 and 16 and the rhythm in bars 7, 21 and 22.

Clarinet quintet

The left hand of the piano should keep a steady beat to guide the melody instrument. The piano plays at a regular speed, but the melody instrument may "bend" the rhythm by playing it slightly slower or faster at certain points. Toward the end, the piano player has to look out for changes of clef in the left hand.

Ave verum corpus

This is a piece for four-part choir. Think of the four notes of the chords as being four voices, to help you imagine how the music should sound. Because the four parts are often moving at the same time, you may need to practice the hands separately at first. Make sure you play slowly - no faster than 50 quarter note beats per minute.

Queen of the Night's aria

The left hand will need practice here because you have to play sustained two-note chords while keeping up a gentle rhythm with your little finger. The grace notes before the sixteenth notes should be hit a fraction before the beat. The aria is for a high soprano, so the repeated notes should be very light and detached. Be careful of the clef change at the foot of the first page.

Important dates in Mozart's life

This chart lists the dates of some of Mozart's most important compositions, as well as other events that took place during his lifetime.

1756 Mozart born in Salzburg
First ever chocolate factory opened in Germany
1759 Voltaire writes *Candide*
Laurence Sterne writes *Tristram Shandy*
General Wolfe captures Quebec
British Museum opened
William Blake (poet) born
George Handel (composer) dies
1760 George III is crowned king of England
F. von Knaus builds first typewriter
1763 First excavations of Roman sites at Pompeii (Mozart visited them in 1770)
1765 Joseph II becomes Emperor in Vienna
1766 Hydrogen discovered by Henry Cavendish
William Pitt becomes English Prime Minister
1768 Mozart composes *La finta semplice*
1769 James Watt develops steam piston engine
First European settlements in California
Royal Cresent built at Bath (see page 13)
Napoleon Bonaparte born
1770 Nicolas Cugnot invents 3-wheel steam car
William Wordsworth (poet) born
Friedrich Hölderlin (poet) born
First public restaurant opened in Paris
Ludwig van Beethoven born
1771 Mozart composes the Divertimento, K113
Walter Scott (novelist) born
First edition of the *Encyclopedia Brittanica*
1772 Mozart composes *Lucio Silla*
Daniel Rutherford discovers Nitrogen gas
Friederich von Schiller (poet) born
1773 "Boston Tea-Party": American sailors tip tea from English ships into sea off Boston, Massachusetts, to protest against the Tea Act
1774 The chemical Chlorine discovered
Joseph Priestley discovers Oxygen
Louis XIV becomes King of France
1775 Mozart writes the Violin concerto, K 219
American War of Independence begins (ends in 1783)
Abraham Darby builds the world's first iron bridge at Coalbrookdale, England
Jane Austen (novelist) born
Alessandro Volta invents the electric battery
J.M.W. Turner (painter) born
1776 Mozart writes the Haffner serenade
American Declaration of Independence from England
Concerts of Ancient Music start in London
Edward Jenner discovers smallpox vaccination

1777 Mozart composes the Piano sonata, K309
1778 Mozart writes the Concerto for flute and harp for the Comte de Guines
La Scala opera house opened in Milan
1779 Mozart composes the *Sinfonia concertante* and the Posthorn serenade
The Velocipede, a forerunner of bicycle, is first seen in Paris
1780 Symphony no.34
Empress Maria Theresia dies in Vienna
Jean Ingres (painter) born
1781 William Herschel discovers planet Uranus
1782 Serenade for 13 wind instruments, K361
1783 Montgolfier brothers invent hot-air balloon
John Broadwood patents piano pedal
1784 First European settlements in Alaska
Pierre Augustin Beaumarchais writes original play of *The Marriage of Figaro*
1785 Mozart composes the String quartet, K465
Edmund Cartwright invents the power loom
Jean Pierre Blanchard invents the parachute, and becomes the first man to cross English Channel by balloon
Alessandro Manzoni (novelist, poet) born
1786 Mozart writes *The Marriage of Figaro*; the Duos for horns, K487; the Piano concerto in A, K488; and the Horn concerto in E flat
1787 Mozart composes *Don Giovanni*; A musical joke; and *Eine kleine Nachtmusik*
The United States of America formed from 13 former British colonies
Britain transports first group of convicts to Australia
Lord Byron (poet) born
Christoph Gluck (composer) dies
1788 Mozart composes the Divertimento for string trio, K563
The Times of London, the first daily newspaper, is published
1789 French Revolution begins
George Washington becomes the first President of the United States
William Blake (poet) writes *Songs of Innocence*
1790 The first lifeboat is built
Discovery of the metallic chemical Strontium
1791 Mozart composes the *Ave verum corpus*; the Adagio and rondo for glass harmonica; and *The Magic Flute*
Mozart dies at five minutes to one in the morning on 5 December
Guillotine introduced in France
Samuel Morse, inventor of Morse Code, born
Franz Gillparzer (dramatist) born
John Keats (poet) born

Glossary

This list explains the Italian musical terms used in this book, as well as some other words that may be unfamiliar. If a word appears in **bold type** within an entry, that word has its own entry in this list.

Adagio Literally, "at ease", slowly. The word is also sometimes used to describe a movement with this **tempo** indication.

Allegretto A little slower than Allegro.

Allegro Fast, lively.

Andante Moderately slow, at a walking pace.

Aria An operatic song.

Arrangement An adaptation of a piece of music. An arrangement can be a simpler version of the original piece, or a new version of it for different instruments.

Cadenza A section for the **soloist** near the end of a **concerto** movement or **aria**. Usually the accompaniment stops, while the soloist plays **virtuoso** passages based on the themes of the piece.

Castrato A male singer whose voice has not broken. Castratos were very popular in the 18th century.

Chromatic note A note other than those in a major or minor scale.

Concerto A work for one or more solo instruments and orchestra.

Crook A detachable piece of tubing that is inserted into a brass instrument to change the tube length.

Divertimento A light-hearted piece for keyboard or instrumental ensemble, usually with between five and nine movements.

Duet, duo A piece for two performers, either with or without accompaniment.

Dynamic, dynamics In a piece of music, the indications of how loud or soft to play.

Form The "shape" of a piece of music, or the way in which it is organized.

Gavotte A lively dance in 2/2 or 2/4 time. The gavotte orginated in France.

Grazioso Gracefully.

Improvisation Making up a piece of music while it is being played. When improvising, the performer composes the piece as he or she goes along. Some improvisations are based on well-known tunes.

Key The most important note of the scale on which a piece of music is based. *also* The part of a piano or harpsichord, usually made of wood or ivory, that the fingers touch.

Legato Connected smoothly, with no break between the notes.

Minuet An elegant dance in 3/4 or 3/8 time. It originated in France.

Movement An individual section of a large piece of music such as a **symphony** or a **sonata**. In most 18th-century music, there is a short break between each movement.

Polonaise A stately processional dance, originally from Poland. Polonaises are usually in 3/4 time.

Presto Fast: faster than allegro.

Rondo A musical **form** in which the main section or theme is played several times. In between, there are sections of different music, often contrasting with the main theme.

Scordatura The retuning of one or more strings on a stringed instrument, either for a special effect or to make passages in difficult keys easier to play.

Serenade A piece for an instrumental ensemble. Played in the evening or on social occasions, serenades had up to ten **movements**. They were often intended to be played outside.

Sinfonia A piece of music used to introduce an opera, or to cover the sound of moving scenery between acts. In the early 18th century sinfonias usually had three **movements**: fast slow fast.

Soloist In a **concerto**, the performer who plays the main melody part, accompanied by the orchestra. The word is also used for a performer playing an unaccompanied piece.

Sonata A piece of music, usually in several movements, for a soloist or small ensemble.

Soprano The highest female voice.

Staccato Detached or separated. Staccato notes are shown by a dot or a wedge, below or above the note-head.

String quartet A group of two violins, a viola and a cello, or a piece of music written for that group.

String trio A group of stringed instruments, usually violin, viola and cello.

Suite A set of musical movements, often dances, grouped together to be played in order.

Symphony A piece for orchestra, usually in three or four movements.

Tempo The speed at which a piece of music is played.

Theme An individual melody in a longer piece of music. In a **symphony** or a **sonata**, there are usually many different themes grouped into movements.

Trio A piece of music for three players. *also* In a **suite**, **sonata** or **symphony**, the second part of a **minuet** movement.

Virtuoso A very skilled performer.

Index

First published in 1993 by Usborne Publishing Ltd, Usborne House, 83-85 Saffron Hill, London EC1N 8RT, England. Copyright © 1992 Usborne Publishing Ltd. The name Usborne and the device 🎈 are trade marks of Usborne Publishing Ltd. All rights reserved.

American edition 1993. First published in America August 1993.